AuthorHouse™
1663 Liberty Drive
Bloomington, IN 47403
www.authorhouse.com
Phone: 833-262-8899

Because of the dynamic nature of the Internet, any web addresses or links contained in this book may have changed since publication and may no longer be valid. The views expressed in this work are solely those of the author and do not necessarily reflect the views of the publisher, and the publisher hereby disclaims any responsibility for them.

Any people depicted in stock imagery provided by Getty Images are models, and such images are being used for illustrative purposes only. Certain stock imagery © Getty Images.

This book is printed on acid-free paper.

Interior Image Credit: Metu Jallow

New International Version (NIV)
Holy Bible, New International Version®, NIV® Copyright ©1973, 1978, 1984, 2011 by Biblica, Inc.® Used by permission. All rights reserved worldwide.

Scripture quotations marked KJV are from the Holy Bible, King James Version (Authorized Version). First published in 1611. Quoted from the KJV Classic Reference Bible, Copyright © 1983 by The Zondervan Corporation.

Amplified Bible, Classic Edition (AMPC)
Copyright © 1954, 1958, 1962, 1964, 1965, 1987 by The Lockman Foundation

ISBN: 978-1-6655-2543-5 (sc)
ISBN: 978-1-6655-2544-2 (e)

Print information available on the last page.

Published by AuthorHouse 05/20/2021

authorHOUSE

Once upon a time there was a beautiful little girl named Chloe' who attended a new school. She was excited and couldn't wait to get to school and meet new friends. Once she got there Chloe' immediately felt uncomfortable being around her classmates. All of her classmates were white, not another Black kid in site. None of them took time to welcome Chloe' or even show her any kind of love. It seemed as though the other kids that attended the school were not friendly at all toward her.

Actually they would not play with her because she looked so much different than the other kids. She feared the other kids treated her differently because she was the new kid at the school. Chloe' never considered that she was treated differently because of the color of her skin. While Chloe' was on the playground she could hear the kids calling her bad names.

They were singing this cruel song while jumping rope. Other kids said nasty things like "why is that black girl going to our school? We can't play with her because we may turn black if we touch her. She should go to a school with kids that look like her." Chloe' has never been exposed to racism and does not know how to respond. Chloe' was so sad and frightened as she left school. Kids yelled at her saying:

"Chloe' Chloe' you are so black
Leave our school & don't come back.
We don't like kids like you
So please go away boo hoo hoo!!"

Chloe' bravely came back to school with a very heavy heart. The kids were all playing some game or another which again did not include Chloe'. They found themselves not being able to play Double Dutch because they did not have enough players. Even though there were lots of kids on the playground there was only one other little girl that wasn't already playing another game that could play Double Dutch and that was Chloe'. They would rather not play Double Dutch than to include her.

She was perplexed because she really did not understand why she was not loved by the other kids and why they chose to call her names. Chloe' had always been taught that she should do everything in love. She knew that true love, the agape love (God's love) would overcome all things. So she continued to love on those hateful kids with the love of God. They continued to be mean girls. She never said anything bad toward them like they did say to and about her.

Instead, Chloe' expended her positive energy as she played with the butterflies that appeared as delicate flowers of the air. These fluttering butterflies had beautifully colored wings as fragile falling petals in the warm wind.

They flew up and down as Chloe' chased them, the only real friends she had. At least the butterflies did not care what she looked like and they couldn't say mean things back to her. The butterflies played with her when the kids would not. These gaily colored butterflies were like fairies fluttering from flower to flower seemed to be receptive to the love that radiated from Chloe's beautiful spirit. She felt the love of God being returned to her even from the butterflies, but yet no love from the kids on the playground.

As weeks and months passed, things did not change on the playground, and Chloe' continued to have faith in the Word of God. Chloe' has been praying and reading more of the Word of God and that changed her view of the situation. If God could cause butterflies to love Chloe', surely He could cause the children on the playground to love her too.

Chloe' Prayed

The Lord is my shepherd; I shall not want. He maketh me to lie down in green pastures: he leadeth me beside the still waters. He restoreth my soul: he leadeth me in the paths of righteousness for his name's sake. Yea, though I walk through the valley of the shadow of death, I will fear no evil: for thou art with me; thy rod and thy staff they comfort me. Thou preparest a table before me in the presence of mine enemies: thou anointest my head with oil; my cup runneth over. Surely goodness and mercy shall follow me all the days of my life: and I will dwell in the house of the LORD forever. Psalms 23 KJV

Amen

Chloe' made up her mind and stopped trying to win them over as friends. She no longer tried to look like the other kids or trying to fit in where she didn't. Chloe came to school rocking a different look and had a different spirit. She was no longer sad or disappointed. She had developed the same spirit as Joshua.

In the Bible it stated that Joshua had a spirit of an overcomer; not being afraid of anything or anyone. Chloe' adopted that same spirit of Joshua. She once looked at the kids on the playground as "giants" who were impossible to be won over as her friends. Kids that were once viewed by her as giants on the playground had lost their power over her all because of the powerful overcoming spirit of Joshua.

Chloe' remembered once reading a story in the Bible about the twelve spies that were sent to scout out Canaan, the land of milk and honey, the land that God had promised the Children of Israel. She had learned that two of the spies (Joshua and Caleb) had a different spirit than the other ten spies who believed the inhabitants of the land were giants and victory could not be accomplished. The ten spies saw themselves as small as grasshoppers being unable to have the victory. She knew there is no victory without faith.

Chloe' then knew that there could be nothing or anyone that would cause her to feel sad about attending school with people that did not accept her for who she is "a beautiful Black child of God." The kids on the school playground began to look at Chloe' in a different way. She was determined to show them that she was a child of the almighty God no matter what her heritage may appear to be in their eye sights. She knew that she could do all things through Christ Jesus who strengthens her.

If you haven't guessed, Chloe' was not being treated badly because she was a new kid on the block as she had originally believed. She was being treated differently because the color of her skin was not like theirs. Chloe' had no idea that people could be so hateful because of the color of a person's skin. She was confused because she was not taught to treat people differently. She was taught to treat others like she would like to be treated.

This was Chloe's first encounter with racial discrimination. She would have been devastated if she did not know the Lord. God's Word gave her strength, confidence and the love that surpassed man's understanding, and filled the gap that was missing in her life. Some of the children felt intimidated and approached her with a fierce conversation about how different she is and how they were to play with the children of your own kind.

They were angry telling her to go back to the school she came from. Those hateful kids said to Chloe', "we do not want to play with you because you are not good enough to play with us." They also told her "You are Black and you are inferior to us and you deserve to live in your own neighborhoods and attend their own schools."

Chloe' did not see herself as being inferior. She saw herself as being the head and not the tail. She saw herself being above and not beneath just as the Word of God said. Chloe' was convinced that she is the righteousness of God in Christ Jesus. Above all, Chloe' knew that she was the light of the world and that she was delivered from the curse of sin, sickness and poverty.

The devil will try any tactic possible to cause division and trouble for a child of God. His job is to steal, kill and destroy any believer that comes into his path. His job is to steal Chloe's joy! So he thought!!! Chloe' is a believer and she knows the power of God. She decided to open her mouth and tell the kids on the school's playground that she has courage and is not intimidated by their rude tactics. Chloe' further told them, "enough is enough! I love people and I want you to be happy with me, but I will not allow you to control me. I am led by the Holy Spirit, so you had better watch out. I do have power!"

Reading the Word of God helped her to be slow to anger. She spoke answers that turned away wrath and did not say grievous words like the other children who were trying to stir up more anger. When the devil could not cause division in his attempt to use Chloe' he tried a different approach. Chloe' continued to display the love of God toward them and they continued their divisive tactics to cause her to leave the school and to miss out on her blessing of a better educational opportunity.

Chloe' had been keeping this problem from her parents since she became a student at that school. Feeling separated, unfairly treated and excluded to no end she still tried to remain as cool and calm as possible. This stress is more than a 7 year old child should ever have to bear.

This situation reminds me of an important moment during the Civil Rights Movement in 1957 when the Black high school kids called the "Little Rock Nine" were racially discriminated against because they wanted to attend an all- white Central High School in Little Rock, Arkansas. The then governor ordered the National Guard to prevent them from enrolling in the school. After all of these years it appears to still be racial discrimination against Black students in this country. Chloe' is a perfect example of how Black students are received and perceived in this country. Racial hatred is still alive and kicking!!

Chloe' finally broke down and told her parents about the abuse she received from the kids at the new school. Her mother was furious and said, "We are going to address this issue with the school administrators. We want to know why they are not protecting you from the wrath of the other kids. This is outright racial discrimination and we will not stand for it."

Meanwhile, mom and dad sat down with Chloe' and had a heart to heart conversation about racism. Her mother told Chloe' that there are people in this world that feel as though they are superior over people of color. Her father also made Chloe' to know that she is a beautiful Black Princess in his eyes and in the eyes of the Lord. God did not make any mistakes when he brought you into this world. You have a purpose in this world and it will not be hindered by the misguided thoughts of others.

There are some that think you are not as good as they are but you are better.

Your mother and I celebrate your uniqueness. Do not allow the words of those mean people hurt you or hinder you. You deserve the same opportunities as those kids that are trying to hurt you. Always remember

that Black is beautiful! You are beautiful! Chloe' was taught to depend on God and not to lean on her own understanding and her mom was ignoring all that she had learned about the Lord. Chloe's mother was angry and chose to take matters into her own hands instead of depending on God. Chloe' on the other hand was displaying strength and courage and her mother was displaying fear for her daughter. Fear and anger allows the enemy to enter into the thought pattern of a person and gives off false evidence appearing real. The treatment that Chloe' endured is real, but the devils so called power is not real.

The Bible says, "As I wait on the Lord, with good courage, He shall strengthen my heart." Psalm 27:14. As Chloe's mother decided to visit the school, Chloe' is praying that the Lord will go with her because she knows that the Lord will not leave her nor forsake her. Chloe's mother met with the school principal who acted like she was not aware of any such treatment. The principal was not supportive at all and had no solution to the problem. It was determined from that meeting that the racial culture of that school is originating from the administrators in charge of making the culture of the school what it is NOW!!

While this meeting was in progress, Chloe' was praying to the Lord for peace. She said, "I am praying to please you God, and I know you have the power to make my worst enemies to be at peace with me." The next day at recess, Chloe' went outside to the playground where she had been yearning for months to play Double Dutch rope with the kids. Although there had been so much push back against her, she still had faith that God would work things out.

Chloe' entered the playground and began to wander around. She watched kids play and they still did not invite her to play with them. She watched another group play basketball and they did not ask her to play with them either.

As she was about to become discouraged and turned to leave the playground some of the kids playing hop scotch asked her why she never played hopscotch with them. Chloe' said, "You are of the same color as the other kids that say mean things to me because of the color of my skin and I thought you felt the same way about me as they do. Those other kids playing Double Dutch were racially discriminating against me and I did not want to endure that treatment from anyone else. I am sorry I thought you were racist also because you are white." They thought Chloe' did not want to play with them, and she thought that since the other kids were so unkind to her that this group of kids were of the same ugly spirit. Chloe' had been patient, endured the test, received God's strength and power to come out of this situation as an overcomer. It was not by her might or her parent's might but by the might of the Lord. She showed the entire school that through faith and patience, she endured and dared to have the boldness, courage and confidence to hope for something that was not seen. No one, not even her parents, expected to see a favorable outcome after speaking with the principal. The principal gave little hope for a resolution of the situation that Chloe' had endured for this entire time.

"HE GIVES STRENGTH
TO THE WEARY
AND INCREASES THE
POWER OF THE WEAK..."

ISAIAH 40:29

The Bible said in James 4:7 "I am submitted to God and the devil flees from me, because I resist Him in the name of Jesus." Chloe' lived by faith and not by sight and God was pleased. God made her an overcomer in spite of all of the obstacles that were in her path.

The very next day the same kids that had treated her so unkind, came to her and asked her to play Double Dutch with them. They apologized to her for their behavior and told her that they were taught by their parents that they should not play with kids of another skin color.

They appeared to be so sorry. Suddenly, all of the kids at the school wanted to become friends with Chloe'.

The love of Jesus brought about a miraculous change in the way they treated Chloe'. She no longer had to lower her standards, hide her culture and play with butterflies instead of real friends. Away with the butterflies!! God gave her real friends. "Let us love one another, for love is (springs) from God; and he who loves [his fellowmen] is begotten (born) of God and is coming [progressively] to know and understand God. He who does not love has not become acquainted with God [does not and never did know Him]" 1 John 4: 7-8 AMPC

Whose report do you believe?

Jesus
Jesus
Jesus